FAMILY TREE

Grace Margaret Nicol (Meg)
(Retired Nurse & Secretary)

M. Hector Archibald McColl
(Butcher – deceased)

GRANMA MAINLAND

James McColl **M.** Rachel Stoddart   Matthew McColl
(Reverend)

Hector McColl   Archie McColl   Dougal McColl   Jamie McColl   Murdo Iain McColl

THE BIG BOY COUSINS

For the island where it all started

JOIN KATIE MORAG ON MORE ADVENTURES . . .

Katie Morag Delivers the Mail
Katie Morag and the Two Grandmothers
Katie Morag and the Tiresome Ted
Katie Morag and the Big Boy Cousins
Katie Morag and the New Pier
Katie Morag and the Wedding
Katie Morag and the Grand Concert

Katie Morag and the Riddles
The Big Katie Morag Story Book
The Second Katie Morag Story Book
Katie Morag's Rainy Day Book
Katie Morag's Island Stories
More Katie Morag Island Stories

Check out www.kidsatrandomhouse.co.uk/katiemorag for more information on Katie Morag and her family and friends, plus some fabbydoo notes for fans everywhere, written by Lindsey Fraser!

KATIE MORAG AND THE BIRTHDAYS
A Bodley Head Book: 0 370 32850 7

First published in Great Britain in 2005 by The Bodley Head,
an imprint of Random House Children's Books

1 3 5 7 9 10 8 6 4 2

Copyright © Mairi Hedderwick, 2005

The right of Mairi Hedderwick to be identified as the author and illustrator
of this work has been asserted in accordance with the Copyright, Designs and Patents Act 1988.

RANDOM HOUSE CHILDREN'S BOOKS
A division of The Random House Group Ltd, London, Sydney, Auckland, Johannesburg and agencies throughout the world.

THE RANDOM HOUSE GROUP Limited Reg. No. 954009

A CIP catalogue record for this book is available from the British Library.

Printed and bound in China

Katie Morag

and the
BIRTHDAYS

Mairi Hedderwick

THE BODLEY HEAD
LONDON

JANUARY

It was a special day on the Isle of Struay; it was Flora Ann McColl's first birthday.

"I remember her being born last year," said her big sister, Katie Morag. "I was jealous, but not any more," she smiled, giving her little sister a kiss and a present. It was a teddy bear made out of an old fur hat that she had found in the dressing-up box. Katie Morag loves making presents. Katie Morag also loves the excitement of other people's birthdays. But each time she can't help asking, "When will it be MY birthday?"

"A long time yet!" replies Grannie Island. "This is only January, the first month of the year. Lots of other birthday months before yours!"

ISLE of STRUAY SHOP & POST OFFICE

January   February   March   April

May   une   July   Au

r   Octo   mber

From
Granma
Mainland

FEBRUARY

Neilly Beag is married to Katie Morag's other grandmother, Granma Mainland. She often gads off to the mainland for a shopping spree in the big city. This time it was on Neilly's birthday. "I'll bring something back for you, darling!" she promised.

"Poor Neilly," thought Katie Morag, "I would hate to be all alone on my birthday."

But she need not have worried. The McColl family, and all the neighbours popped in to wish him "Happy Birthday".

"A ceilidh!" cheered Grannie Island. Secretly, she was glad that Granma Mainland was not on the island; the two grandmothers don't always see eye to eye with each other.

"WHEN is it MY birthday?" Katie Morag asked, wishing it was right NOW.

"Patience!" smiled Mr McColl. "Only three months to wait."

"That's a LONG time," sighed Katie Morag, but she smiled a bonny smile as she got up to dance a birthday jig for Neilly. Presents don't always have to be made or bought.

70 Years Young

To Neilly Love from atie orag xxx Feb 10

MARCH

March is the birthday month of all the sheep on the Isle of Struay. They huddle together in the shed to keep warm from the freezing winds and wait patiently for their lambs to be born.

Alecina, the naughtiest of the sheep, but Grannie Island's favourite, had disappeared. Grannie Island was angry and worried at the same time. "Wait till I catch her!" she frowned. For days Katie Morag and her grandmother trekked over the moors in the wind and the sleet calling Alecina's name. Even Bob, Grannie's dog, couldn't find her.

Finally, one very snowy day, they found her. There she was with her very own present to herself – the first lamb of the spring!

"You old devil!" scolded Grannie Island, but she was smiling. "Sheepcake birthday cake for you when we get back home!"

"I'm glad I'm not a lamb, even a birthday lamb," shivered Katie Morag. "WHEN is it MY birthday, Grannie Island?"

"When it is warmer and sunnier; in exactly one month and fourteen days," said Grannie Island. She is very good at sums. "Will I make you a sheepcake birthday cake, too?"

"Ugggh! No thank you!" laughed Katie Morag.

APRIL

Liam always wakes up very early on his birthday. His big sister was at his bedside with a COLOSSAL parcel in her arms. The rest of the family were still sound asleep.

"Open it!" said Katie Morag, bossily. There was another parcel inside and then another . . . and ANOTHER . . . and ANOTHER! Liam ripped the paper off the diminishing parcels with squeals of delight. But the very last and very tiny parcel had NOTHING in it!

"April Fool!" teased Katie Morag. Liam's sad little face burst into tears.

That woke the rest of the household.

"Someone is at the door, Katie Morag," called Mr McColl, from her parents' bedroom. "Maybe it is Grannie Island." Katie Morag raced to the door but there was no one there.

"April Fool!" chanted her mum and dad.

Now Katie Morag knew what it felt like and she decided never to try that trick again on someone smaller than herself. She quickly found Liam's real present: a trailer for his tractor.

For once, Katie Morag didn't pester her parents by asking, "WHEN is it MY birthday?" Instead, she spent the day helping her little brother set up his model farm. She remembered that her birthday is not long after Liam's. It is NEXT MONTH . . .

To Liam

Liam April 1st

. . . THE MONTH OF MAY! Yes! Katie Morag's very own birthday month!
But it isn't just HER birthday on a day in May – would you believe it, she shares
it with both her grandmothers! The day before, Katie Morag makes cards for them.

TO MAKE CARDS, KATIE MORAG NEEDS:
two pieces of stiff card • mug • eggcup • scissors • pencil and rubber • paints or
felt-tip pens • one birthday candle • glue • small, white or gold doily • gold and
silver stars • glitter glue, ribbon, feathers, jewels and anything else you fancy

Grannie Island's Birthday Card

1. Fold the card in half

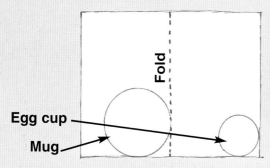

Egg cup
Mug

2. On the back, draw around the mug on
the bottom right-hand edge of the fold

3. On the front, draw around an egg cup
on the bottom right-hand edge of the card

4. Draw the tractor

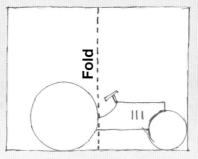

5. Cut out the back wheel to where it
meets the fold top and bottom

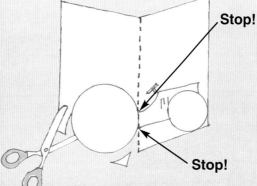

Stop!

Stop!

*As well as a tractor,
you could make
a digger, a bicycle
or a racing car.
Remember to have
the same size circles
for the wheels of the
bike and the car!*

6. Colour in the tractor and stick on a
birthday candle for the exhaust

7. Write your message on
the front and inside
of the card

To Grannie
Island

Happy
Birthday

Granma Mainland's Birthday Card

1. Fold the card in half

2. Place the mug on the top edge of the fold and draw around it

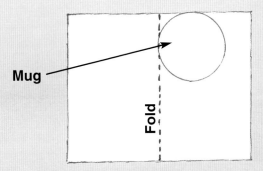

3. Cut out a circle to where it meets the fold top and bottom, as shown

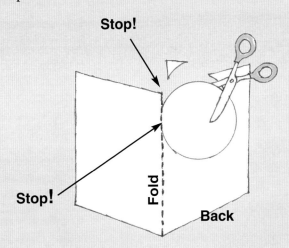

4. Cut off the top of the back of the card to make a straight edge, as shown

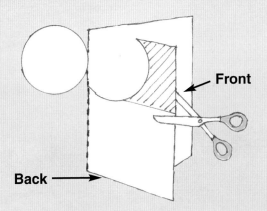

5. Stick the doily to the circle and decorate with ribbons, stars, glitter or whatever you fancy

6. Write your message on the front and inside of the card

Granma Mainland's card could be made into a balloon, a flower, a moon or even a face!

MAY

"How many HOURS till my birthday?" Katie Morag asks when Mrs McColl tucks her up in bed.

"As many hours as it takes for the moon to go round the house," replies her mother. "Go to sleep and the time will pass quickly."

But Katie Morag couldn't sleep; she kept imagining what her presents might be, and how many, and will she LIKE them . . .

TO: Katie Morag
The Shop & P.O.
Isle of Struay
Scotland

SPECIAL DELIVERY

She watched the moon travel ever so slowly across the windowpane and wondered if her two grandmothers were wide awake, too. And then she wondered if any other children far over the sea from the Isle of Struay shared her name day. Maybe one day she would find out and meet them.

Granma
Main land

Grannie Island

She was so excited she couldn't sleep, but she must have drifted off, because suddenly . . .

Grannie
Island

Granma
Mainland

May 2nd

It's HERE . . . Katie Morag's BIRTHDAY! Liam had to pull the
bedcovers off her bed to wake her up. "Happy Birthday to you . . ."
and "For she's a jolly good Katie . . ." the whole family sang together.
Grinning, Katie Morag took lots of time to carefully unwrap and
unknot each parcel. "Hurry up!" cajoled her little brother.
Liam hasn't yet learned that slow unwrapping is much more
exciting. She left the biggest and the smallest parcels to the end.

  Her grandmothers brought two parcels; one soft, one hard.
There was also a big card. It said:

HAPPY BIRTHDAY
Love
from Mum & Dad
x   x

TO: Kat
The Sh
Isle
Sc

Love from
Uncle
Matthew
x

*The Two Grandmothers invite Katie Morag
to The Bistro tonight. No wellie boots. RSVP*

"Yes, please!" cried Katie Morag, jumping out of bed and
giving her grandmothers their presents. Then she rushed off
to try on her new frock from Granma Mainland and the little
pointy shoes from Grannie Island.

Invitation

From Grandad Island ☺   AIRMAIL

SPECIAL DELIVE

TO MISS MCCOLL — Love from
Uncle James, Aunt Rachel
and the Big Boy Cousins
x x   x x x x x

LOVE FROM X
NEILLY BEAG

Katie Morag, Granma Mainland,
Grannie Island May 2nd

That evening, sitting very upright and posh in the Bistro, Katie Morag decided it was a great thing to be able to share her birthday. Especially with her grandmothers. Not many granddaughters can do that.

The large cake on the sideboard had a candelabra on top holding three gold candles. "Ladies never tell their age," explained Granma Mainland. So that's why Katie Morag keeps her age a secret, too.

She hoped the beautiful grown-up night would go on for ever because it would be a WHOLE YEAR before her next birthday. But she looked forward to wearing her wellies the next day. Shoes can be very uncomfortable if you are not used to wearing them.

Soup of the Day
~
COCK A'LEEKIE SOUP

The Bistro
TICOAT TAILS
EW RASPS

Happy Birthdays
to the Girls

123

Katie Morag's Castle Cake for Birthdays or any time!

YOU WILL NEED:

- 6oz (170g) butter • 2 eggs
- 5oz (140g) icing sugar
- 1½ oz (45g) cocoa powder
- 2 packets of plain, square or rectangular biscuits

CLEANING OUT THE BOWL IS THE BEST BIT!

First, line an eight-inch cake tin with greaseproof paper — draw round the base for the bit that will line the inside bottom of the tin. Then, cut pieces a bit higher for the sides (so it is easier to pull the cake out later).

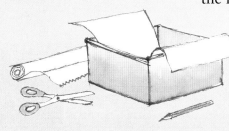

TO MAKE THE CHOCOLATE MIX:

1. Ask an adult to help you melt the butter. Leave to cool
2. Whisk two eggs until fluffy (get help with the mixer)
3. Add the icing sugar
4. Add the cocoa powder
5. Mix all the ingredients above together

Save some biscuits and chocolate mix for the four towers to be added later!

TO ASSEMBLE THE CAKE:

1. Fill the tin with one layer of biscuits and then one layer of chocolate mix, all the way to the top, starting and ending with a chocolate layer. Chill the cake

2. When firm, CAREFULLY turn out the cake onto a plate or board covered in silver foil
3. Add towers
4. Chill again while you make the decorations

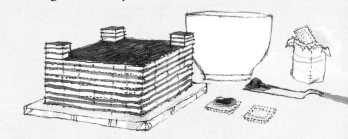

TO MAKE THE DECORATIONS:

PEOPLE CAKE BAND

1. Fold a piece of A4 paper twice broadwise

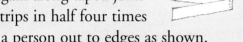

2. Cut along each fold
3. Tape short sides together

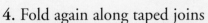

4. Fold again along taped joins
5. Fold strips in half four times
6. Draw a person out to edges as shown. Keep arm ends quite fat!

7. Cut around the figure but NOT at the end of the arms

Do not cut here! → ← **Do not cut here!**

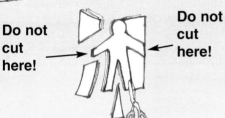

8. Gently pull out the chain of figures and decorate with faces and pretty princess frocks. Use silver foil for knights in shining armour
9. Wrap around the cake

Use extra long candles for flaming torches. Ask an adult to help you light them!

FLAGS

1. Cut rice paper into flag shapes
2. Paint on patterns and friends' names with a fine brush and food colouring
3. Pierce cocktail sticks in and out of one side of each rice paper flag. Stick a glacé cherry, marshmallow or a gooey sweet on top of each one
4. Decorate your castle with flags

TELL YOUR FRIENDS THEY CAN EAT THEIR NAMES!
They won't believe you!

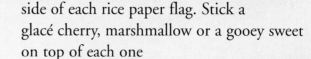

Sasha

me

Flora Ann

Murdo Iain

Hector

Sophie

Agnes

Dougal

Kirsty

Archie

Liam

Erika

Jamie

Sam

Ewan

JUNE

Litters of kittens and puppies are born on the same day. Katie Morag's cats, Fabbydoo and Mr Mistake, are two of Scratch Patch's SEVENTH litter.

"And now she's had more!" wails Mrs McColl, who has a terrible time trying to find homes for the kittens. "And no, we CANNOT keep them," she tells Katie Morag.

June is also the birthday month of Katie Morag's twin uncles, Sven and Sean. They are world-famous musicians who live in London. They come to Struay to celebrate their birthdays. Guess what presents Katie Morag gives her uncles this year?

Katie Morag doesn't dare ask her parents, "WHEN is it MY birthday?" so soon after her birthday, but she asks Fabbydoo and Mr Mistake. They just miaow and twitch their whiskers and say not a thing. They know it will be a very, very long time. Longer than it will take for their half brothers and sister to get to their new home in London.

Uncle Sven and Uncle Sean June 19th

JULY

The Big Boy Cousins were all born in the same month too, but in different years. Except for the twins, Jamie and Murdo Iain, of course. Their older brothers, Hector, Archie and Dougal, celebrate different days in the month. Katie Morag finds it REALLY difficult to remember whose birthday is when!

The Big Boy Cousins and their parents have come to live on the island. The islanders gave them a welcome barbecue at the Old Castle.

"Let's have a day like this every year!" cheered Hector.

"We'll call it the Anniversary of our Arrival!" said Archie.

Dougal, Jamie and Murdo Iain agreed wholeheartedly.

"Make it a joint party for ALL your birthdays as well," suggested Katie Morag.

And that is how July 14th became an annual anniversary and birthday event on the Isle of Struay. Everyone is invited.

After games on the beach and a treasure hunt in the Castle, the best bit is the barbecue, but even then Katie Morag can't resist asking the Big Boy Cousins, "WHEN is it MY birthday?"

Ready for THE question, they chorus in reply: "NINE MONTHS, TWO WEEKS AND TWO DAYS!"

The Big Boy Cousins are very good at sums, too.

"That is FOR EVER . . ." sighs Katie Morag.

AUGUST

One person who often forgets her birthday is Mrs McColl. And so does everyone else for that matter, because it is in August, the busiest time of the year. Not only does Mrs McColl have to run the Post Office and deliver the mail during the day, she has to serve in the Bistro at night and, in between, clean the Holiday House for the visitors and then help her husband stock the shelves in the Shop with the supplies that the big boat brings from the mainland.

Katie Morag knows to keep well out of the way at times like this and not dare to ask THE question but she still thinks it inside her head. "WHEN will it be MY birthday . . . ?"

Show Day is quite the most hectic day of all. The judges hand out cups and rosettes for the best items that the islanders make and grow. Despite being so exhausted, Mrs McColl always sits up late decorating bottles with shells to enter into the Handicrafts Class.

This year her birthday is on Show Day and she has won first prize!

"Happy Birthday!" said Katie Morag, giving her mother HER first prize in the Children's Class.

Mrs McColl won't forget her birthday this year, will she?

Pets' Corner

Mrs McColl August 5th

How to Make Katie Morag's Presents:

THE MINIATURE GARDEN

1. Ask an adult for a large plate to build your garden on
2. To make the pond, you will need silver foil
3. For the grassy bits, dig up real earth and grass or use playdough painted green
4. To make the fence, use spent matchsticks and thread. Ask an adult for help!

Matchstick Fence

5. For flowers, use real daisy heads or make your own paper flowers
6. To make the bushes, tease out half a cotton bud and paint it green
7. Make a wavy path with tiny gravel or (uncooked!) rice or lentils

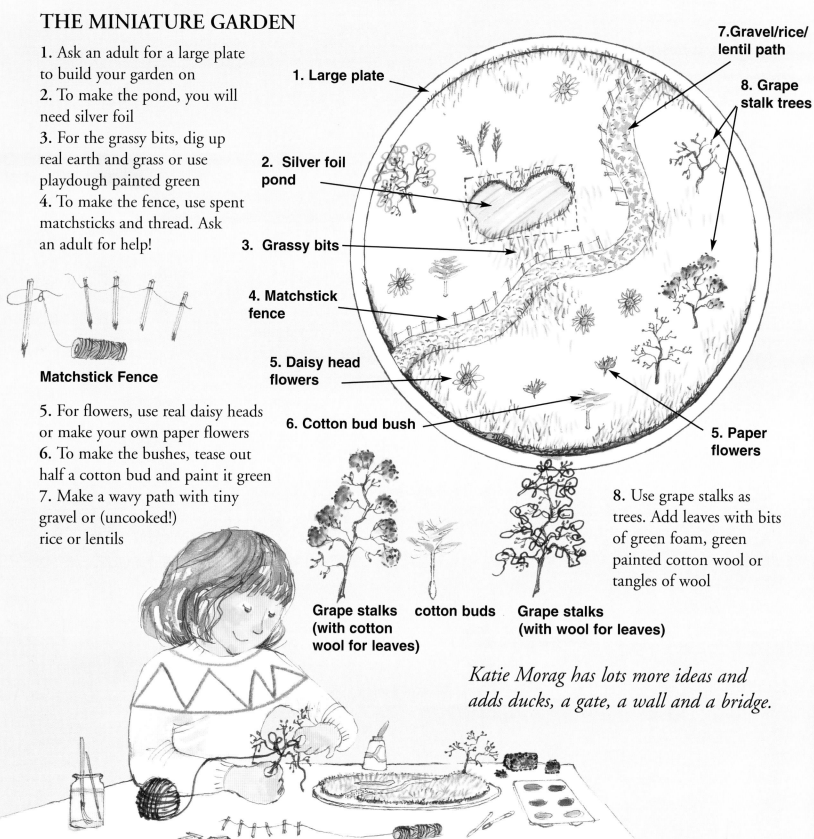

1. Large plate

2. Silver foil pond

3. Grassy bits

4. Matchstick fence

5. Daisy head flowers

6. Cotton bud bush

7. Gravel/rice/lentil path

8. Grape stalk trees

5. Paper flowers

Grape stalks (with cotton wool for leaves)   cotton buds   Grape stalks (with wool for leaves)

8. Use grape stalks as trees. Add leaves with bits of green foam, green painted cotton wool or tangles of wool

Katie Morag has lots more ideas and adds ducks, a gate, a wall and a bridge.

A DESK TIDY FOR GRANNIE ISLAND OR GRANMA MAINLAND

WHAT YOU NEED
toilet roll tube • two empty matchboxes • card •
two folder hinges • scissors and strong glue

1. Glue two matchboxes together side by side
2. Cut out two pieces of card slightly
bigger than the top of the joined matchboxes
3. Stick the card on the top and bottom of
the matchboxes
4. Glue the toilet roll tube on to the top
of the matchboxes

5. Ask an adult to help you make
a hole in front of each matchbox
and thread through one half of
the folder hinge to make a
drawer pull

6. Decorate with
whatever
you like –
fancy or simple

*Katie Morag made a REALLY fancy
one for Granma Mainland!*

OUTRAGEOUS SUN SPECS FOR MR McCOLL

WHAT YOU NEED
Beg, borrow (but don't steal) an old pair of sunglasses •
gold or silver stars • can ring-pulls • coloured wool •
beads/macaroni • Post-Its™ • felt-tip pens • glue

1. Thread beads/macaroni onto long lengths of coloured
wool. Tie onto little ring-pull holes. Make lots of these!
2. Slip larger ring-pull holes over the arms of the glasses
3. Cut two square Post-Its™ into triangles with the
sticky bit on the bottom, as shown.
4. Take two more square Post-Its™, cut a frilly edge
into one side of each square (opposite the sticky side),
and stick onto the triangles, as shown
5. Decorate with glitter and colour
with felt-tip pens. Stick onto the top
of the sunglasses

*Stick gold or
silver stars round
the edge of the
lenses to decorate*

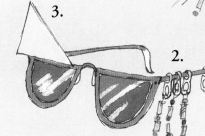

Mr McColl will look like a superstar!

SEPTEMBER

Once a year, on his brother Matthew's birthday, Mr McColl walks over to the other side of the island to pay him a visit.

Uncle Matthew lives all on his own in a hut with a cat and a parrot. He grows his own food; the hens and the goat give him eggs and milk.

"He's a hermit!" says Mrs McColl.

"He's just a bit shy," says Mr McColl.

Katie Morag knows what it feels like to be shy.

Katie Morag hands Uncle Matthew his present. He smiles a big smile when he opens the Joke Book.

"What do you get if you cross a cat with a parrot?" He reads out loud.

"A carrot!"

Everyone bursts out laughing.

On the way back home, Mr McColl tells Katie Morag stories about when he and his brother were little. "Matthew is two years and a month older than me so he looked after me. Just like you look after Liam." Katie Morag nodded. "This is the month of September, so which month is my birthday, Katie Morag?"

"Oh, dear, Oh dear!" thought Katie Morag to herself. "WHEN is it MY birthday?" But she concentrated hard and answered, "Next month?"

"Well done!" smiled Mr McColl, amazed that Katie Morag had not asked THE question.

What do you get if you cross a parrot with a ? A !

OCTOBER

Mr McColl's birthday is on Hallowe'en. On that wild scary night on the Isle of Struay the grown-ups go round the houses in disguise as well as the children. Mr McColl loves dressing up.

As long as Katie Morag stays close to him, Liam likes Hallowe'en. This Hallowe'en, Katie Morag and Liam were going round the Village, knocking on doors and reciting "The Riddle of the Cow", trying not to giggle at the rude bit:

> *Four stiff-standers,*
> *Four dilly-danders,*
> *Two lookers,*
> *Two crookers*
> *And a wigwag.*

Katie Morag's torch showed up some weird and wonderful guisers weaving along the Village Street. It was very scary not knowing who anybody was – except for Mr McColl. He was wearing the fancy sunglasses that Katie Morag had given him for his birthday.

Do you know, Katie Morag never asks once about her birthday on Hallowe'en. I wonder why?

Mr McColl October 31st

NOVEMBER

Looking forward to a big birthday party can be very tummy tickling, but some of the best birthday parties can be had with just two or three people. There is a particularly quiet and private party on the Isle of Struay on November 5th with just two guests and a dog.

On that day Katie Morag walks over to Grannie Island's cottage with a large bone in her rucksack. Is it for Grannie to boil for tea? Of course not! It is for Bob, Grannie Island's dog. It is his birthday.

"I remember it well," reminisced Grannie Island. "His mother had six pups and he was the last. Just as he was born the fireworks started going off. Ever since, he's been terrified of loud bangs. I never leave him alone on his birthday."

Katie Morag is more than a wee bit frightened by fireworks, too. She and Bob like to sit on the windowsill and watch the brilliant display of dazzling lights and flashes exploding far away, on the other side of the Bay.

When the fireworks are over and Bob has finished his bone, Katie Morag just has to ask THE question, "WHEN is it MY birthday, Grannie Island?"

"Five months and twenty-seven days," Grannie Island replies. "Best to forget about it. Bob does."

"I wish I were a dog," sighs Katie Morag.

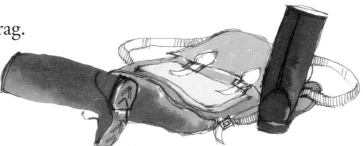

DECEMBER

Everyone knows what is so special about the twelfth and last month of the year. Christmas is on the 25th day – presents for EVERYONE!

"But it is also the birthday of someone special who lived thousands of years ago," Grannie Island reminds everyone.

On Christmas Eve, the McColl family parcel up their presents and decorate the house. Then they listen for the sound of Grandad Island's helicopter. He always visits the island on Christmas Eve and brings the most unusual presents from all over the world.

"For your birthdays as well as Christmas," he smiles.

"But WHEN is it YOUR birthday?" Katie Morag decided to ask this Christmas time.

"I don't have birthdays," laughed Grandad Island.

He took Grannie Island, Katie Morag and Liam up for a whirl round Village Bay in his helicopter. Christmas tree lights twinkled in the houses below just as the first stars came out up above.

Soon it was time for Grandad Island to leave.

"Happy Birthday, Santa Grandad!" Katie Morag called out into the dark, blue sky.

December

"Grandad Island must have a birthday some time – like me and everybody else," yawned Katie Morag at the end of Christmas Day. But she has to ask THE question.

"WHEN is it MY birthday? How MANY months and days?"

"None! This is the last month of the year!" said her mother and father ever so seriously.

"Oh dear," sighed Katie Morag. "Working out birthdays is so complicated. Like Bob, I'll just forget about them."

"No you won't," smiled Grannie Island. "Here is an extra Christmas present. It is a birthday book. You can write down everyone's birthday date and never forget."

Wide-awake now, Katie Morag blew Grannie Island a kiss and a hug as she ran to bed with her new treasure. She would put her name in first, for sure.

"Thank goodness, Katie Morag won't have to ask, 'WHEN IS IT MY BIRTHDAY?' ever again!"

Mr and Mrs McColl smiled at each other, much relieved.

"THANK YOU VERY MUCH, GRANNIE ISLAND!"

1	9	17	25
2	10	18	26
3	11	19	27
4	12	20	28
5	13 *Flora Ann*	21	29
6	14	22	30
7	15	23	31
8	16	24	

1	9	17	25
2	10 *Neilly Beag*	18	26
3	11	19	27
4	12	20	28
5	13	21	29
6	14	22	
7	15	23	
8	16	24	

1	9	17	25
2	10	18 *Alecina*	26
3	11	19	27
4	12	20	28
5	13	21	29
6	14	22	30
7	15	23	31
8	16	24	

1 *Liam*	9	17	25
2	10	18	26
3	11	19	27
4	12	20	28
5	13	21	29
6	14	22	30
7	15	23	
8	16	24	

1	9	17	25
2 Katie Morag, Grannie Island & Granma Mainland	10	18	26
3	11	19	27
4	12	20	28
5	13	21	29
6	14	22	30
7	15	23	31
8	16	24	

1	9	17	25
2	10	18	26
3	11	19 Uncle Sven & Uncle Sean	27
4	12	20	28
5	13	21	29
6	14	22	30
7	15	23	
8	16	24	

1	9	17	25
2	10	18	26
3	11 *Jamie & Murdo Iain*	19	27
4 *Hector*	12	20	28
5	13	21	29 *Archie*
6	14 *Anniversary of Arrival Day*	22	30
7	15	23	31
8 *Dougal*	16	24	

1	9	17	25
2	10	18	26
3	11	19	27
4	12	20	28
5 *Mrs McColl*	13	21	29
6	14	22	30
7	15	23	31
8	16	24	

1	9	17	25
2	10	18	26
3	11	19	27
4	12	20 *Uncle Matthew*	28
5	13	21	29
6	14	22	30
7	15	23	
8	16	24	

1	9	17	25
2	10	18	26
3	11	19	27
4	12	20	28
5	13	21	29
6	14	22	30
7	15	23	31 *Mr McColl*
8	16	24	